WAYANS FAMILY PRESENTS

THUG A BOO™

SNEAKER MADNESS

SCHOLASTIC INC.

New York   Toronto   London   Auckland   Sydney
Mexico City   New Delhi   Hong Kong   Buenos Aires

ISBN: 0-439-74598-5

10 9 8 7 6 5 4 3 2 1   6 7 8 9 10

Printed in the U.S.A.
First printing, September 2006

CHAPTER 1
MISS ATTITUDE

The ground shook as Slim took off running toward the pool.

"Here comes the cannonball!" he shouted.

D-Roc and the rest of the Boo Crew stood back as Slim launched his jelly belly into the air.

SPLASH! The water flew straight up into the air, then came crashing down in the pool again.

"Cannonball? That was more like a meteor, Slim!" said D-Roc.

The rest of the Boo Crew all laughed and went back to swimming.

It was the last day the pool was open.

School was starting in one week, and they weren't going to waste another second of summer vacation.

"Man, this is how you do it," D-Roc said. "When my rap career blows up, I'm going to buy Momma and Daddy a big house. Then all we're going to do is swim, eat candy, and write rhymes all day!"

His little sister, Dee Dee, laughed.

"Yeah, your rap career is going to blow up all right," she said, "because you're going to bomb at every show!"

The Boo Crew laughed.

D-Roc tried to ignore his sister and began to rap.

"Yo, check it . . . this is D-Roc, coming off the dome,
I just threw on my hat, didn't use a comb. Got on the
fly sneakers for the honeys and peeps. Gonna bump
the cool music in my brand-new . . . my brand-
new . . . *car*?"

"JEEP!" everyone yelled.

"SMOG ALERT!" Gwenny shouted.
"Dirty's getting in the pool."

Dirty walked onto the diving board with a
cloud of dust trailing behind him.

He bounced twice, then dove into the pool.

The clear blue water turned oily black right away.

"That's gross!" Gwenny said. "Why don't you go
take a bath?"

"What do you think I'm doing now?" Dirty smiled.

Everyone in the pool swam away.

Just then, the Boo Crew heard the loudspeaker
come on. A grouchy, sassy voice started to speak.

"Oh, great! It's Miss Attitude," Chad said.

"I know you are all aware that today is the last day of our summer program," she said. "That means the pool will be closing. That means, NO MORE SWIMMING!"

Suddenly, two men ran over to the pool, reached in, and pulled out a huge plug.

All of the water quickly drained out.

Miss Attitude's voice came back on.

"Now, I hope you all had a very fun summer, but it's time to get out of here. I'm tired of looking after you. SHOO!"

"Awesome! Now I can totally skate the pool," said Chad. He jumped on his skateboard, hit a bump and went flying.

"Chad, are you OK?" the Boo Crew called.

"I'm fine. It's just a bump on my arm," he said.

"See you next summer, pool!" D-Roc said as they left. All the kids were upset.

Summer was definitely over.

MONEY The Cartoon

CHAPTER 2
THE GOLDEN ISSUES

The Boo Crew walked home.

"Well, that's it. School starts next week," D-Roc said.

"I can't wait to go back," Dee Dee said.

"Why?" asked Chad.

"Because going back to school puts me one step closer to becoming the first female president," she said.

D-Roc laughed. "You can't be president—with your big mouth, you'd blab out all of our top secret information!"

"Whatever!" Dee Dee said.

"I can't wait to go to school so I can go to acting class, dance class, and singing class, 'cause I'm a triple threat!" Lissette said with excitement.

"You're right, we are scared of you doing all three!" teased Dee Dee.

"Well, I can't wait to go school shopping,"
Gwenny said. "My mom is taking me to Eco-Bean to
buy a soy jacket, a soy shirt, and leather pants
to match!"

"Leather pants?" asked Dee Dee.

"Well, do you want me to freeze?" asked
Gwenny.

"I can't wait to educate that freight and push them
new skates," Dirty said.

They all stared at him.

"What are you saying?" they asked.

"He said he can't wait to get some new sneakers,"
D-Roc explained.

Dirty smiled at them.

He pointed to a pair of sneakers in a store window.

"Those are hot!" they said.

Right away, they all saw the new Air Jared
sneakers.

There was no doubt about it. The new Air
Jareds were the coolest shoes they had ever seen.

"I want a pair of those!" D-Roc said.

He was sure they would make him the coolest kid
in school.

Shoes like that would even get Diane Johnson, the girl of his dreams, to notice him.

"I have to get those shoes!" he said.

"D-Roc, you must be sleeping!" Dee Dee said.

"Why?" asked D-Roc.

"'Cause you're dreaming if you think Momma's gonna buy you those shoes!" answered Dee Dee.

D-Roc knew his little sister was right.

But he had to have those shoes.
He would have to talk Momma into it somehow.

CHAPTER 3
SHOPPING SUPERSAVER'S

The next morning, D-Roc was getting ready to go school shopping.

Momma had promised to take him and Dee Dee to buy clothes.

D-Roc was ready, but Momma was busy doing what she loved to do best, talking on the phone. She had already been on that phone for hours.

"Mom, are we going shopping?" D-Roc asked.

"Can't you see I'm on an important phone call?" she asked him and kept talking. "Yeah, girl, I'm sorry you got the wrong number, too, but it was nice meeting you."

"But you said you would take us after we finished all of our chores," D-Roc said.

"Did you wash up?" she asked.

D-Roc nodded.

"Did you clean your dirty room?"

D-Roc nodded.

"Did you feed your dog?"

D-Roc shook his head.

"Well, go feed the dog, then we'll go," Momma said.

"Done!" he announced.

Momma was still on the phone. She could talk forever.

In fact, she took the phone with her when
they left.

She was still talking when they got to the mall.

"That cord must go on forever. I don't know why
she doesn't just get a cell phone," D-Roc whispered to
Dee Dee.

"Because they don't make batteries that last as long
as her conversations," Dee Dee added, and they
both laughed.

"Where are we going?" Dee Dee asked.

"I know the perfect store, baby. They're having
a big sale!" Momma told them.

D-Roc was glad, because he knew Momma had
to save money if she was going to buy him the
new Air Jareds.

They walked through Messy's department store
and went down the escalator.

And down.

And down.

And down.

THIS FLOOR BARGAIN
BASEMENT BARN
⬅ NEXT FLOOR : CHINA

Until they finally reached the Bargain
Basement Barn.

"Okay, we're here," Momma finally said and
put the phone in her purse.

Inside the store, the kids were all standing
to the side.

In the middle of the room, there was a
swarming cloud. D-Roc could only see feet
and clothes flying around.

The parents were all wrestling over clothes.

Momma stretched her arms and legs and
warmed up to get in.

"OK, D-Roc, you like baggy jeans, and Dee Dee, you want a pink dress. Hand me my shoulder pads and mouth guard, I'm going in!" Momma said and dove into the crowd.

She came out a few minutes later with a dress torn in half for Dee Dee.

"But, Momma, it's torn in half!" Dee Dee cried.

"Good, then they'll take half off!" Momma said before diving back into the scuffle.

Seconds later, Momma came out with a pair of pants for D-Roc.

"Here, D-Roc, try on these pants," said Momma.

"HEY! THOSE ARE MINE!"

After a long time, D-Roc and Dee Dee finally had a big pile of clothes.

Momma sighed. "Well, I think we're done for today."

"But I still haven't gotten my sneakers," D-Roc told her.

D-Roc grabbed Momma's arms and dragged her all the way to the shoe department.

He held up a brand-new pair of Air Jareds.

"Those are nice. How much are they?"
Momma asked.

"Check this out, Momma," D-Roc said. "These shoes
have double pump action, extra ankle support, Velcro,
air-padded insoles, and the logo changes
colors! Watch these moves, Momma!"

D-Roc put on the Air Jareds and took off
running around the shoe store.

"That's nice, baby, but how much do they cost?" asked Momma.

"One hundred and fifty dollars . . ." D-Roc whispered.

Momma's mouth dropped open and her hair stood straight up on top of her head.

"One hundred and fifty dollars!" she cried. "Do you know all the things I could buy with a hundred and fifty dollars? Four pairs of house shoes, six wigs, a toaster, three French hens, two turtle doves, and a partridge in a pear tree!"

She told him she knew where he could get the same
exact sneakers for five dollars.

"The same exact sneakers?" asked D-Roc.

Then she took D-Roc and Dee Dee to
Johnson's Supermarket, where they had the biggest,
ugliest sneakers D-Roc had ever seen.

They were so ugly that they placed them in the
meat section right next to the pork chops.

"But those aren't Air Jareds, those are Air
Johnsons!" D-Roc frowned.

"I know they are Air Johnsons," said Momma.

"Who is he and what team does he play for?" asked D-Roc.

"He doesn't play for anyone, he is the owner of the supermarket," Momma replied.

D-Roc frowned.

"I'm sorry, honey," Momma said, "but we just can't afford to spend a hundred and fifty dollars on one pair of sneakers."

D-Roc sighed and looked down at the great white marshmallows he would be wearing for the rest of the year.

MONEY The Cartoon

CHAPTER 4
FRIGHT NIGHT BEFORE SCHOOL

On his bed, D-Roc laid out his new school clothes.

A big smile crept across his face. He was going to look good in his new gear.

But then D-Roc looked at the awful sneakers next to his clothes. He could see his reflection in the big ugly shoes.

31

"These are gonna make me big, all right," he said to himself, "the biggest geek in school." Then he had an idea.

Maybe he could get rid of them.

If he lost his sneakers, then Momma would have to buy him the new Air Jareds.

D-Roc picked up the shoes and walked over to the window. He reached back and threw them as hard as he could.

"Done!" he said.

But as soon as he said it, the big ugly sneakers came bouncing back through the window.

"Oh, great," he said. D-Roc was stuck with them.
"Boomerang shoes, I shoulda known."

D-Roc thought maybe the sneakers wouldn't be so
bad once he'd worn them in.

So he put the sneakers on and went to sit
outside.

He looked down at his feet.

The sneakers looked huge in the daylight.

D-Roc began to imagine his first day at school.

"Hey, D-Roc, are you OK?" a voice said.

D-Roc came out of his daydream to find Soo Young standing in front of him.

"D-Roc, hello? Why do you look so down?" she asked.

"Because of these cheap old things. I HATE them," he told her, pointing at his shoes.

"They're not that bad," Soo Young said.

"I wanted the new Air Jareds," he said, "but my momma bought me these 'Air Balloons!'"

Soo Young's eyes lit up. She gazed at D-Roc's sneakers and started to search through her bag.

"I can make those look like Air Jareds," she said.

"How?" D-Roc asked.

"Don't worry, just give me those sneakers. I will have your Air Jareds for you tomorrow."

CHAPTER 5
CLASS ACT

The next day was the first day of school.

D-Roc put on his best blue jersey, which matched his blue Boo York cap and his jeans, with his brightest white shirt underneath.

He was all ready, but Soo Young hadn't given him his new sneakers yet.

Then there was a knock on his window.

Soo Young was on the fire escape.

"OK, sneakers all done," she said.

They looked just like the Air Jareds in the store window.

"WOW!" he shouted.

"How'd you do it?" he asked.

"Ancient family secret." She smiled.

"How can I repay you?" D-Roc took the new sneakers off and put on his old pair.

"IOU!" Soo Young answered as she slapped D-Roc's hand with a piece of paper.

D-Roc couldn't wait to get to school now.

He was going to have the coolest shoes in the entire class.

He ran downstairs where Dee Dee was doing her hair.

She noticed his sneakers right away.

"Where did you get those Air Jareds?" she asked.

D-Roc laughed. "Soo Young made me these from my ugly Air Johnsons!"

"Oooooh, D-Roc, you're going to be in big trouble!" said Dee Dee.

"Why? Just look at all the money I saved Momma." D-Roc smiled. "How could she be mad at that?"

On their way to school, they picked up D.J. and Dirty.

"Those sneakers are hot! They're the most sickest, illest, banannerest, flavorfull-ness joints I've ever seen!" D.J. said when he saw D-Roc.

"You mean you like them?" asked D-Roc with a confused look in his face.

D.J. answered politely, "Yes, they are super neat-o . . . er, I mean those are fresh."

When they got to school, everyone was showing off
their new clothes.

But the kids couldn't take their eyes off of
D-Roc's new sneakers.

Kids came running up to him.

"How in the world did you talk your mom
into buying those?" everybody asked.

"Well, it wasn't easy, but I worked out a deal
that even she couldn't resist," D-Roc told them.

"What kind of a deal?" Slim asked. "I want
a pair."

"Yeah, me too!" another kid shouted.

Soon everyone was shouting "Me too," even
the teachers!

D-Roc's eyes lit up with dollar signs. He had an idea.

"All right, all right, everyone listen up!" D-Roc announced. "Anyone who wants Air Jareds, just give me five dollars now and twenty dollars tomorrow when I deliver the new sneakers."

"Ooh, I'm telling Momma," said Dee Dee. "Come on, Dee Dee, I'll make you a pair for free if you don't tell," pleaded D-Roc.

"Deal!" Dee Dee said, and they shook hands.

Then D-Roc turned to the Boo Crew and said, "OK, we're meeting tonight at the clubhouse after school. I'm going to let you in on a big secret."

CHAPTER 6
SHOES FOR SALE

Soo Young was running around the clubhouse.

"Twenty-five pairs of sneakers! I can't do that by myself," said Soo Young.

"But we're all here to help you," D-Roc told her.

"You've got all the help you need, as long as dinner will be served," said Slim.

"Well, OK. I'll do my best!" she said.

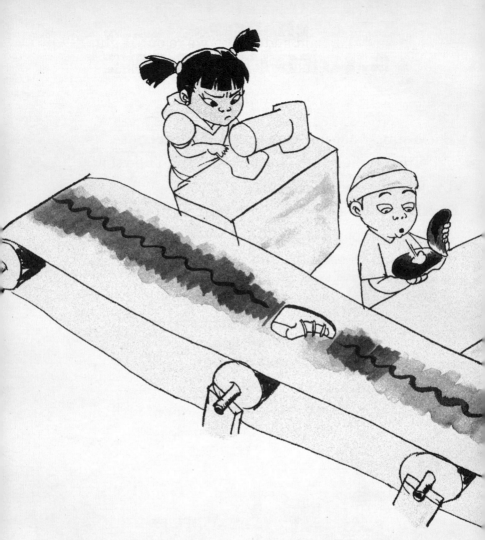

The Boo Crew split up to get the materials they
needed for the shoes.

When they got back to the clubhouse, Soo Young
had them sewing, pasting, and measuring each shoe as
fast as they could.

"Uh-oh," D.J. said suddenly, "we're out of glue."

"Use anything that will stick," Soo Young
told them.

"OK," D.J. said. He spit out his gum and
used that.

Slim used honey.

Dirty picked his nose and used a sticky booger.

The whole Boo Crew worked all night long.

When the sun came up, the sneakers were all finished.

There was a crowd waiting outside the clubhouse.

Even the gym teacher was there. He bought two pairs!

The entire school was lined up to see the new sneakers.

One by one, D-Roc gave out the fake Air Jareds. One by one, students gave D-Roc their money.

D-Roc and Soo Young smiled at each other while they collected and counted their cash.

"This was the best idea ever," he said.

MONEY The Cartoon

CHAPTER 7
UNSTITCHED AND UNGLUED

That day, everyone was wearing their new sneakers.

One kid was walking down the street when honey started to drip from his shoes.

That's when a swarm of bees started chasing him. It wasn't long before the whole school had twisted ankles and swollen feet.

At school, the gym teacher was wearing his new shoes, too.

He was showing his students how to climb a wall with a rope.

"The key is to make sure your feet are properly planted," he said.

As he began to climb, the class heard a squishy sound.

Suddenly, climbing the rope was a struggle, and halfway up the rope, his shoes stuck to the wall.

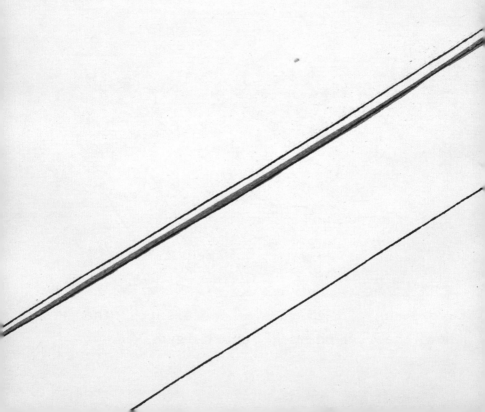

The more he pulled to get them off the wall,
the more they stuck. Finally, he pulled with all
of his might, and his shoes exploded!

The gym teacher's feet were covered in wet gobs of
green slime. The gooey mucus was so slippery that he slid
down the rope and crashed onto the gym floor.

Angry parents started phoning the school.

They demanded the principal do something.

They wanted the kids who sold the sneakers to get punished.

Principal Eyeverson did, too. His feet were also bandaged and swollen from the present that the gym teacher had given him that morning: a new pair of Air Jareds!

Principal Eyeverson knew exactly who was responsible.

An announcement came over the school loudspeakers: "D-Roc and Soo Young, please report to Principal Eyeverson's office immediately."

When they got there, the principal looked mad!

"Now, you two are straight-A students and I know you will tell me the truth—who made these shoes?" the principal demanded.

"I did," Soo Young said.

The principal glared at her.

"Young lady, a lot of kids and some grown-ups were hurt," he said. "I'm calling your parents right now."

D-Roc stood up.

"It wasn't her fault," he said. "I asked her to make them. It's my fault."

"Then you, young man, are in BIG trouble," said the principal. "I've got fifty angry parents who want the student to blame for this sneaker madness expelled from school."

D-Roc didn't want that.

"Maybe I could talk to them and apologize," he said.

He was sure they would understand if he told them the truth.

At least, he hoped they would understand.

CHAPTER 8
A CURIOUS
CONFESSION

Outside the school, it looked like a mob scene. Tons of angry parents with their injured children were waiting out front.

Then there must have been a million other people gathered behind them.

Even all of the local news stations had shown up to cover the apology.

D-Roc could see that they were very, very angry.

It was not going to be easy to get out of this.

The crowd quieted down when they saw him.
They couldn't wait to hear what he had to say
for himself.

"First off," D-Roc said, "I would like to apologize to anyone who got hurt."

He cleared his throat.

"I was just trying to fit in and feel good about myself on the first day of school," he said. "I didn't mean for anyone to get hurt."

"My friend took my ugly sneakers and made them look cooler," D-Roc admitted. "And since my sneakers were such a big hit, I thought that I could make a little money and help other kids feel cool, too.

"I'm really sorry. I've learned that it's not what you wear or how you look on the outside that matters, but who you are on the inside that counts."

The crowd was quiet.

"Oh" —D-Roc remembered something— "and I'm giving everyone their money back."

The crowd cheered.

That's what they wanted to hear.

Dee Dee came up to D-Roc.

"I'm really proud of you, big bro," she said.

"Thanks," D-Roc told her.

"Don't worry," she said, "you did the right thing."

D-Roc knew his sister was right. It was the right thing to do, even if it wasn't what he wanted to do.

As D-Roc looked down, his shoes had fallen apart, too. They looked just as ugly as the day he got them from Johnson's Supermarket.

"Hey, nice shoes!" someone said.

D-Roc turned to find Diane Johnson, the girl of his dreams, standing next to him.

"You got those at the supermarket, right?" she asked.

D-Roc nodded.

"That's my daddy's market, and you're the only one to ever buy his sneakers," she said.

"Really?" D-Roc asked.

"Yeah, so why don't you put those sneakers to use and walk me to class?" Diane said.

D-Roc smiled.

Maybe those big goofy sneakers weren't so bad after all. In fact, now those goofy sneakers made D-Roc feel like the coolest kid in school.

MONEY The Cartoon

THE END